Disney's
My Very First Winnie the Pooh™

Pooh's Honey Hunt

Written by
Lindsay Morgan

Illustrated by
Josie Yee

SCHOLASTIC INC.

New York Toronto London Auckland Sydney
Mexico City New Delhi Hong Kong Buenos Aires

Published by Scholastic Inc., 90 Old Sherman Turnpike, Danbury, CT 06816
by arrangement with Disney Licensed Publishing.

SCHOLASTIC and associated logos are trademarks
and/or registered trademarks of Scholastic Inc.

ISBN 0-7172-6569-2

Printed in the U.S.A.

One day in the Hundred-Acre Wood, Winnie the Pooh and some of his friends had gone to Pooh's house and played together all morning. They'd told stories, they'd played games, and they'd sung songs.

"I wonder what we should do now," said Pooh.

"Hmmmm! Think. Think. Think." He looked as if he were concentrating very hard.

"You really don't have any ideas, Pooh?" asked Piglet.

"Wait!" said Pooh. "Maybe I do."
"What is it?" asked Piglet hopefully.
"My idea is that I always get my best thoughts while I'm eating honey," said Pooh. "So why don't I have a little snack, and then I'm sure I'll think of something."

"Well, let's find you some honey, then," exclaimed Christopher Robin.

"But I don't know how to find honey," said Piglet.

"Hunting for honey is *not* something tiggers do best, either," agreed Tigger.

"We might not have to hunt for it," said Christopher Robin. "Pooh, do you have any honey here in the house?"

"As a matter of fact, I think I do, Christopher Robin," answered Pooh.

"Alright then, everyone," said Christopher Robin. "Let's start our search in the cupboards."

"Good thinking," replied Pooh. "If I were honey, that's the very place I would be!"

So Pooh opened up the cupboard, and everyone took a peek.

"Goodness gracious, Pooh!" exclaimed Piglet.

"Hoo, hoo hoo! I've never seen such a mess of honey pots," said Tigger.

"Really, Pooh! So many pots! What do you need that many for?" asked Christopher Robin.

"I never know when I might get rumbly in my tumbly," answered Pooh. "I try to always be pre-pared for such an occasion by keeping lots of honey around. It's just that the honey never seems to *stay* around."

"Well done, Pooh," replied Christopher Robin. "It looks as if all that planning ahead worked. There should be plenty of honey here for you to snack on."

So the four friends looked through all of Pooh's jars. When they were done, Christopher Robin said, "Pooh, there's barely honey in any of these pots."

"I guess my tummy has been *very* rumbly lately," said Pooh with a smile. "Oh, bother. What should we do now, Christopher Robin?"

"Well, I guess we'll have to go hunting for honey after all," Christopher Robin replied.

"We'll all help," agreed Piglet.

"Why don't we take some hunting tools to help us?" suggested Christopher Robin. Everyone agreed that this was a splendid idea. "It's all settled then. We'll all run home and grab our tools, and meet back here in a little while."

"Please hurry. My tummy is getting more rumbly by the minute," said Pooh.

Then suddenly, he remembered something. "Wait!" he called out. But everyone had left. "Oh bother," said Pooh. "I had something else to tell them."

Soon Piglet arrived at Pooh's door, pulling a cart full of honey-hunting tools. "Phew!" exclaimed Piglet. "I sure hope I brought enough."

"Why, Piglet," said Pooh, opening the door.
"What's all that in your cart?"

"I wasn't sure what to bring, Pooh," replied Piglet. "So I brought *everything*. Do you think any of it will help?"

"Well, actually. . ." Pooh began.

But Piglet was so excited, he didn't wait for Pooh to finish. "I brought a pinwheel to blow the bees the away," he said breathlessly, "a scarf to wrap around your face to protect you from bee stings, an umbrella in case it rains, and . . ."

Just then, Tigger came bouncing up with his own cart full of honey-hunting tools.

"Hi-dee-ho!" shouted Tigger.

"Hello, Tigger," said Pooh. "I was just about to tell Piglet that we don't ..."

"I wasn't exactly sure what we would need, buddy boy," Tigger interrupted, "so I just brought *all* this stuff. I've never been on a honey hunt before!"

"What's in *your* wagon, Tigger?" asked Piglet.

"I brought a tennis racket to swat the buzzing bees with, a teapot for making some tea later to go with the honey, a balloon to help you get up the tree, some spare wheels in case one of the wagon wheels breaks, and a few other odds and ends," Tigger replied.

"But Tigger, Piglet, we don't really need any of those things," explained Pooh.

Tigger was disappointed. "I'm sorry ol' buddy!" he said. "I tried my very best to come up with something."

"Me too," agreed Piglet.

"I suppose I should have explained earlier *how* I hunt for honey," said Pooh.

"Do we need to find some different tools?" wondered Piglet.

"We don't need any tools at all!" announced Pooh.

"You mean Piglet and I brought all of this stuff and we don't even need it?" asked Tigger.

"I'm afraid so," Pooh admitted.

"Well, then ol' buddy, tell us. How *do* you hunt for honey?" asked Tigger.

Just then Christopher Robin came walking up the path. "So is everyone ready to go honey hunting?" he asked.

"Tigger and I brought a whole bunch of stuff for the hunt," explained Piglet. "But after talking with Pooh, it seems we don't need any of it!"

"So, what *do* we need for the honey hunt?" asked Christopher Robin.

"My tummy and some empty pots," replied Pooh.

"WHAT?" exclaimed Tigger and Piglet.

"When I hunt for honey," explained Pooh, "I just follow my tummy. It always gets extra loud and rumbly when honey is nearby."

"Okay, so now we know how we'll find the honey," said Piglet. "But how will we bring it home?"

"We could use a net—I think I have one in here somewhere!" said Tigger. He began to dig excitedly through his wagon.

"But the honey will pour right through the holes," Piglet pointed out.

"All we need are honey pots," said Pooh. "I just reach into a tree, scoop out the honey, and put it into the pots. Then taste a little, of course."

"But that's so easy!" exclaimed Tigger. "Why didn't I think of that?"

"'Cause you're not a Pooh bear!" Christopher Robin replied.

Everyone laughed and began to pile Pooh's empty pots into a cart. Then off they went, listening extra closely for Pooh's tummy to rumble its way straight to some honey.

P.S. And that's how Pooh and his friends spent the afternoon, after wondering what they would do next!